A Note to Parents and Caregivers:

Read-it! Joke Books are for children who are moving ahead on the amazing road to reading. These fun books support the acquisition and extension of reading skills as well as a love of books.

Published by the same company that produces *Read-it!* Readers, these books introduce the question/answer pattern that helps children expand their thinking about language structure and book formats.

When sharing a book with your child, read in short stretches, pausing often to talk about the pictures and the meaning of the book. The question/answer format works well for this purpose and provides an opportunity to talk about the language and meaning of the jokes. Have your child turn the pages and point to the pictures and familiar words. Read the story in a natural voice; have fun creating the voices of characters or emphasizing some important words. And be sure to reread favorite parts.

There is no right or wrong way to share books with children. Find time to read with your child, and pass on the legacy of literacy.

Adria F. Klein, Ph.D.
Professor Emeritus
California State University
San Bernardino, California

Managing Editor: Bob Temple
Creative Director: Terri Foley
Editor: Sara E. Hoffmann
Designer: John Moldstad
Page production: Picture Window Books
The illustrations in this book were prepared digitally.

Picture Window Books
5115 Excelsior Boulevard
Suite 232
Minneapolis, MN 55416
1-877-845-8392
www.picturewindowbooks.com

Printed in the United States of America.

Library of Congress Cataloging-in-Publication Data
Dahl, Michael.
Rhyme time : a book of rhyming riddles / written by Michael Dahl ;
illustrated by Garry Nichols ; reading advisers, Adria F. Klein,
Susan Kesselring.
p. cm.—(Read-it! joke books)
ISBN 1-4048-0227-4
1. Riddles, Juvenile. I. Nichols, Garry. II. Title.
PN6371.5 .D347 2003
818'.602—dc21

2003004870

Rhyme Time

A Book of Rhyming Riddles

Michael Dahl • Illustrated by Garry Nichols

Reading Advisers:
Adria F. Klein, Ph.D.
Professor Emeritus, California State University
San Bernardino, California

Susan Kesselring, M.A., Literacy Educator
Rosemount-Apple Valley-Eagan (Minnesota) School District

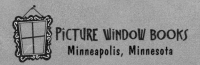

PICTURE WINDOW BOOKS
Minneapolis, Minnesota

What do you call a skinny bird?

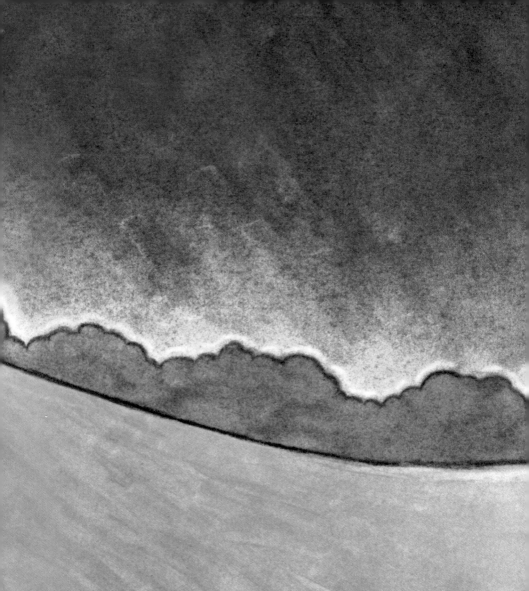

A narrow sparrow.

What does a little cat wear on its paws in the winter?

Kitten mittens.

What do you find
on a wet envelope?

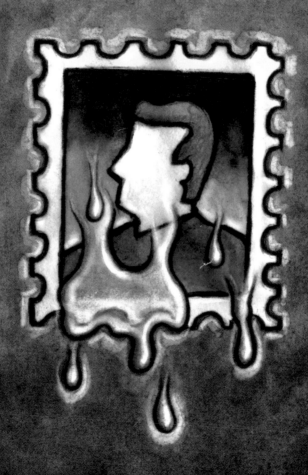

A damp stamp.

Where does a snail go when it breaks the law?

Snail jail.

What kind of rain makes the garden grow?

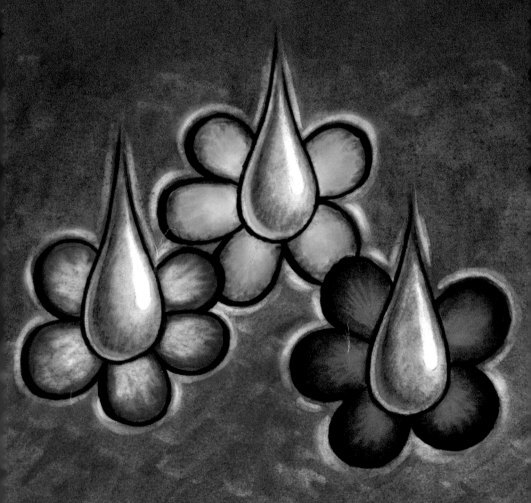

A flower shower.

What do you call a gecko with magical powers?

A lizard wizard.

What kind of medicine do you take when you're seasick?

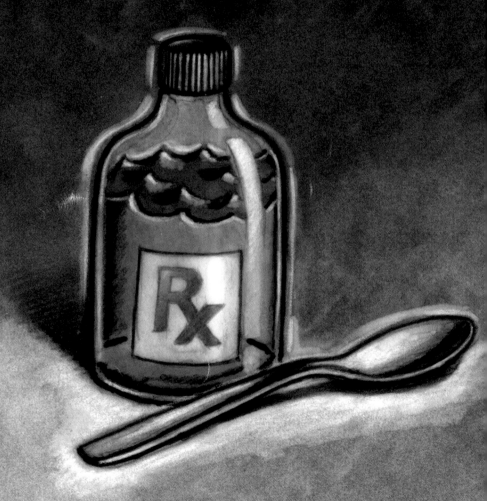

An ocean potion.

What do you call a little hen with a cold?

A sick chick.

What flashes in a scary
thunderstorm?

14

Frightening lightning.

What do you call a crate full of stockings?

A socks box.

How does a reptile tell time?

With a croc clock.

What do you call a rabbit that tells jokes?

A funny bunny.

What does a humpback get from the post office?

Whale mail.

What do you call a sticky old Egyptian king?

A gummy mummy.

What do you call a lamb that doesn't like to spend money?

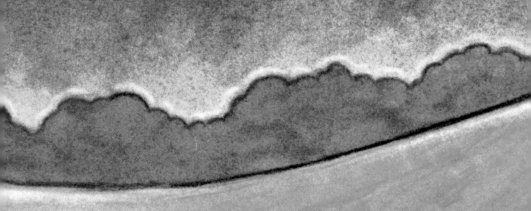

A cheap sheep.

What sound does a hog make when it sleeps?

A boar snore.